The Book of Numbers

ISBN: 978-1963424102

Library of Congress Cataloging _ In Publication Data Moore, E.
The Book of Numbers/by E. Moore

For more information about
The Book of Numbers, visit:
www.myakids.com

The Book of Numbers
Written & Illustrated
By E. Moore

author website
www.ebonymoore.com

1

one

2
two

3

three

4

four

5

five

6
six

7

seven

8

eight

9

nine

10

ten

How many of these Mya books have you read?

Fire Safety with Roy

When My Parents Argue

When I am Sad

When I Believe

The Book of Shapes

Earning and Saving Money

and many more...

Visit

www.myakids.com

for additional books and products.

www.ingramcontent.com/pod-product-compliance
Lightning Source LLC
Chambersburg PA
CBHW041416300726
48978CB00002B/112